THE
FAVORITE
BOOK

For Adam

Candlewick Press, 99 Dover Street, Somerville, Massachusetts 02144. visit us at www.candlewick.com.
Printed in Shenzhen, Guangdong, China. 19 20 21 22 23 24 CCP 10 9 8 7 6 5 4 3 2 1

THE
FAVORITE
BOOK

Bethanie Deeney Murguia

Candlewick Press

How do you choose
a favorite, a best?

Which would you pick
before all the rest?

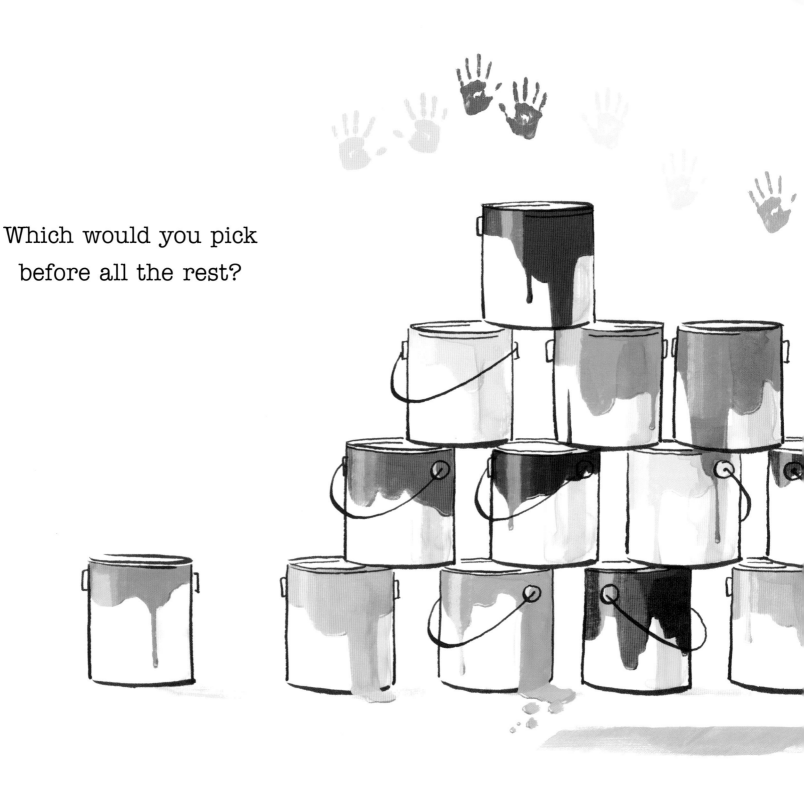

Do you examine,
determine, inspect,

measure, and weigh before you select?

Or do you just know
right from the start?
You may be the sort
who follows your heart.

What gets your vote?

Which is the one?

Maybe you'll realize
your favorite is . . .

NONE!

Or what if just one
couldn't possibly do?

Can you pick two
or three?

Well, that's up to you!

Do you follow along
and go with your friends?

Or are you the type who starts your own trends?

A favorite can be
a way to connect.

A favorite can change . . .

if you re-select!

Some favorites choose us
to be in their crew.

And then before long . . .

we're choosing them, too.

The favorites we pick, the choices we make,
become part of us and the path that we take.

And always ahead, more favorites await.

Wonders to find, and to create.

From here to the sea to the sky up above—
there are so many things in this world you can love.